Fly
Blanky
Fly

For Patrick, who launched his blanky and yelled, "Fly blanky fly!"
Love always,
Mom

For my little sister, Vanina
—E.C.

Fly Blanky Fly

Written by Anne Margaret Lewis • Illustrated by Elisa Chavarri

HARPER

An Imprint of HarperCollinsPublishers

One night before bed, a boy and his blanky stood towering at the very top stair. With a giant heave-ho and a very big throw, he launched it with might through the air.

This was the night Sam's adventures began with a daring and boisterous cry. From the top of his lungs to the pit of his belly, Sam roared a loud…

"FLY BLANKY FLY!"

Zoom, zoom...like a jet flying through the sky.

ZOOM BLANKY ZOOM!

Whooshing to the moon like a rocket so high.

Hippity-hopping like a bouncing kangaroo.

HOP BLANKY HOP!

Trotting and marching like a camel through the zoo.

MARCH BLANKY MARCH!

Spreading your wings like a proud butterfly.

FLY BLANKY FLY!

Slithering through the trees like a snake so sly.

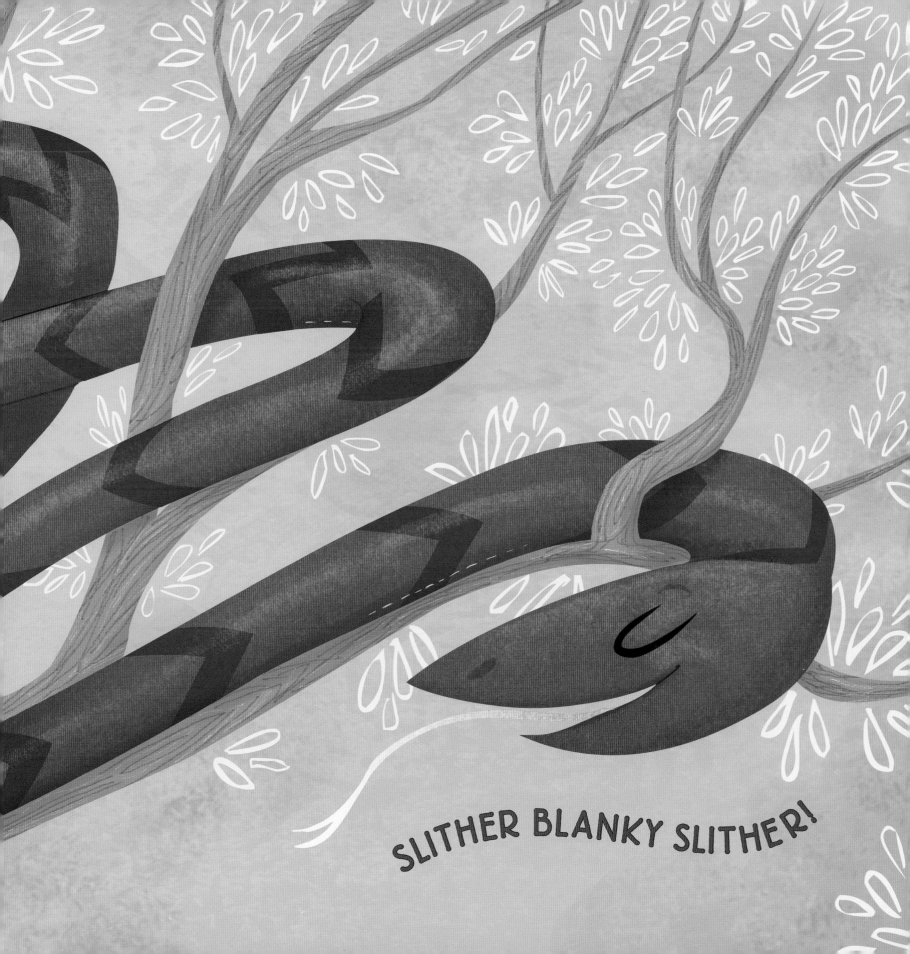

SLITHER BLANKY SLITHER!

Swishing through the spout of a giant humpback.

Choo-choo-ka-chooing, chuggin' down the track.

Whirling through the sea like a shimmery sea horse.

Gliding and sailing like a boat on course.

GLIDE BLANKY GLIDE!

Playing in the stars and swingin' on the moon.

SWING BLANKY SWING!

Snoozing and snoring, napping till noon.

At last, it was time
for Sam to count sheep.
He whispered so quietly,

"Sleep blanky sleep."

Library of Congress Cataloging-in-Publication Data is available.
ISBN 978-0-06-199996-3

Typography by Jeanne Hogle
12 13 14 15 16   SCP   10 9 8 7 6 5 4 3 2 1
❖
First Edition